CW00555064

THE IMLEN BRAT

THE
IMLEN
BRAT

SARAH AVERY

PUBLISHED BY
Point Quay Press
2001 Veirs Mill Road #233
Rockville, MD 20848

Copyright ©2016 Sarah Avery
Cover Art Copyright ©2016 Kate Baylay
Interior Art Copyright ©2016 Kate Baylay

ISBN (trade paper): 978-0-9974140-2-8
ISBN (ebook): 978-0-9974140-3-5
ISBN (audiobook): 978-0-9974140-4-2
All rights reserved. No part of this book may be reproduced, scanned or distributed in print or electronic form without the express, written permission of the author.
This is a work of fiction. Names, characters, places and incidents are the product of the author's imagination and any resemblance to any organization, event, or person, living or dead, is purely co- incidental.

Cover Design: Design for Writers
Interior Design: Design for Writers

ILLUSTRATIONS

For the whole Black Gate crew — writers, readers, artists, editors, all of you. You will always be this story's first home.

ACKNOWLEDGEMENTS

This novella became a book because John O'Neill, who had acquired it for *Black Gate*, gave me a crucial bit of encouragement. When *Black Gate* stopped publishing fiction before "The Imlen Bastard," as it was then titled, came up in the queue, John said it had always troubled him to pay so little for such a good story, and that he was certain I could get it the attention it deserved if I published it on my own. The story had done me the kindness of coming to me to get written, so I set out to keep faith with it.

Betsy Mitchell's developmental edit showed me where the manuscript needed more clarity and force. It's one thing for a novella to be the centerpiece of a magazine issue, and another for it to stand alone as a book. Betsy also allowed me to invoke the rock-solid credibility of her name in my Kickstarter campaign, without which no book would have been possible. And she helped me give the book a title that would open doors, after I had given it a title that would close them. I will always appreciate her brilliance, patience, and kindness.

The first time I saw Kate Baylay's work was the moment I knew exactly what I wanted my cover art to feel like. When she agreed to take on my project, I could barely believe my good fortune. Of all the joys this project has brought me, seeing my fictional world through Kate's eyes has been one of the greatest.

Hearing that world through the voice of C.S.E. Cooney, my audiobook narrator, has been another of those greatest joys. What started out as a question about how to make my work more accessible to a visually impaired fan, and then to friends and relatives with dyslexia, turned into the chance to hear my characters interpreted anew, some in ways I never anticipated.

My critique group, Writers of the Weird, workshopped several sections of the manuscript in its early stages. The long-manuscript sub-group we experimented with workshopped the entire novella. WOTW has a more permeable, more mutable membership than most critique groups, which makes it almost certain that my list of particular thanks will miss some people who should be on it. First, always, I owe thanks to David Sklar, who introduced me to the group. David and his wife Rachel Young both read and commented on multiple drafts of *The Imlen Brat*. Phil DeParto — our host, moderator, and impresario — was indispensable. Pauline J. Alama, Pat Fitz-Nash, Richard Herr, and Peter Gutierrez all offered important advice, as well.

Gregory Frost and Darrell Schweitzer led a workshop session at Philcon in, I think, 2006, where they helped me prepare the manuscript for its first submission. If they had not told me how close it was to ready, it might still be in a file folder titled "Half-Abandoned Bits."

My first draft of this book began its life as a National Novel Writing Month project in 2005. I had been writing seriously for many years at that point, but the wild enthusiasm of NaNoWriMo helped me detoxify after years in academia. Chris Baty, who runs the whole crazy show, and the many local volunteers who organize write-in events will always have my appreciation.

When finally I was ready to crowdfund the project, I drew on the experience of many people who knew more about Kickstarter and self-publishing than I did. Scott Taylor, Patty Templeton, Andrew Plotkin, and several of my fellow broads on the Broad Universe email list helped me get my bearings. Levi James and Ian Anderson generously allowed me to try their crowdfunding course for musicians, Launch + Release, to see how it might apply to authors. If I had done nothing else to prepare for Kickstarter, that course would have been enough, and I wish I'd figured out sooner that my geeky fantasy fiction project was, for purposes of crowdfunding, more like a band's first indie album than it was like a game designer's first indie game. Many friends and colleagues helped me get the word out, especially John O'Neill, that encouraging editor and publisher of *Black Gate*.

The people who made it possible for me to bring this book into the world as its best possible self — the people who empowered me to hire Kate Baylay to give it a face, Claire Cooney to give it a voice, and Betsy Mitchell to give it a diploma — are the hundred and three Kickstarter backers who supported my campaign. I'm grateful to them all, including the ones whose real or full names I do not know: Akua, Day Al-Mohamed, Amy, Theresa Anderson-Kentner, Bruce Avery, David Avery, Marisa Avery, Peggy Avery, Jennifer Barker, Coty Behanna, Marek Benes, Lara Beneshan, Richard Berman, Maria Blaeuer, Bard Bloom, Christopher Bogs, Elizabeth Brunt, Matt Callahan, David Carlson, Catalina Castells, Sabrina Chase, Laura Cherry, Laurie Christiansen, David Conklin, Charlotte Crerar, William Crosbie, Abigail Daken, Dan Davis, Daniel B. Davis, Betty Day, Chris Day, Laura Day, Arinn Dembo, Clare Deming, Vickie DiSanto, Ivo Dominguez, Jr., Christopher Dunnbier, Sarah Elkins, Emilyc15, James Enge, Sean Forbes, Madhavi Ghare, Rachel Goldsmith, Nicole Gustas, Jennifer Hamilton, Zachary Herz, Karen Hoofnagle, Joseph Hoopman, Lee Howard, Rebecca Hranj, Scott Hungerford, Iulian Ionescu, Laura Johnson, Amy Juviler, Anna Kashina, katre, Anne Mushin Kaufhold, Justin Kim, Amy Knoch, Alicia Korenman, Angela Korra'ti, Ariel Landau, Kelly Lasch, the Lennhoff family, Seth Lindberg, Lisa, William Lohman, Gregory Lynch, Mary M., Phil Margolies, Patricia Matson, Aleecia

McDonald, James McKendrew, Michael Mooty, Tom Murphy, Joshua Neff, Dale Newfield, Steve Peterson, Andrew Plotkin, Bill Racicot, Rebecca, Robert, Shauna Roberts, Dave Rostker, Karen Schmeelk-Cone, Rene Sears, David Sklar, Andrew Silverman, Hildy Silverman, Martha Smith, Eric Snider, Cindy Lynn Speer, Marijah Sroczynski, Maggie Stewart, Ian Stockdale, Sumoslap, Emily Townsend, Prudence Upton, David vun Kannon, Amy Williams-Scott, Dorothy Weaver, Janice Wing, and Sally Wright.

My family in all its forms — nuclear, extended, in-law, and might-as-well-be — rallied around this project, and around me while I was working on it. Often I find that what drives my characters is the lack of some blessing that's present in my life. Stisele, our heroine in these pages, yearns to be supported as she is by the family she has. Her family struggles to do that, and whether they succeed is open to debate. Mine can, and has, again and again. In particular, my husband Dan Davis and our sons Gareth and Conrad cheered me on through every stage of bringing this book into being. My thanks and love belong to them, always.

Never before had Stisele of Imlen got herself in so much trouble. Not the time she caught the drapes on fire in the nursery when she modified Samren's toy catapult. Not the time she pulled the chandelier down in Mommy Utroneth's antechamber behind the throne room by pretending it was ship's rigging. Not even the night she knocked Jrene off the dock and into the sea for making fun of her imaginary friends. That had made Mommy Utroneth angry enough to yell at her, and Mommy Utroneth didn't like yelling. Now here Stisele was in the antechamber again—the chandelier was all better now, like nothing ever happened—and Mommy Utroneth was deciding what to do with her.

By the door to the throne room, Stisele's imaginary friends huddled to listen. Flash and Blur were way better at listening than Stisele was. *Utroneth's not even in there,* said Blur as the diffuse brightness of her slid down to the floor, where she drifted into a patch of sunlight on the figured carpet. *I don't understand.*

Flash bounced against the ceiling in agitation. *If Emnir's in there, and Utroneth isn't....* He didn't finish his thought, and Blur didn't take it up.

"What?" said Stisele.

Nothing, the two imaginary friends said.

Hang on, said Flash. *Someone's in there with Emnir.*

So Stisele and Blur hung on for what seemed like forever, until Flash said, *Stand up straight, Stisele. They're coming.*

She would have liked to ask him who, but there was no time. Flash skittered out of the way of the door as it swung open, and there in the frame stood Emnir of Gorsae in his dress blacks, the silver insignia of the Order gleaming on his chest, and behind Emnir, a man Stisele had never seen before. It was hard to read the stranger's uniform because she kept being distracted by his enormous moustache, but Stisele thought he was from the House of Ythrae's troop levy.

"They say you fight dirty when you play Pirates with the other children, Stisele," said the man with the big moustache. "Is it true?"

Stisele glanced over to the corner where Flash and Blur hovered, a mottling of golden light against the dark wooden paneling, but they didn't have any advice for her. So she looked back at the stranger, hoping he didn't notice how she turned to her imaginary friends. Everyone kept telling her she'd outgrown them. "I didn't mean to," she said. "Emnir, you saw. I didn't mean to cut Jrene. I didn't."

Mommy Utroneth's bodyguard said, "Yes, I saw."

The big moustache man turned to Emnir. "Describe it."

"The heir had a small wooden practice blade, nothing very sharp. Jrene started a game of Pirates and Commoners, and Stisele was a commoner."

"Like always," Stisele muttered.

"*As* always," Emnir corrected her. "Stisele pulled Jrene's practice blade away from her and was quick enough to cut her with it. No edge, just speed. Her Royal Highness's children have been getting lessons for two years now. Such lessons were, of course, not planned for Stisele, but it seems she may have a useful aptitude."

The man with the moustache walked around Stisele, looking her over. His uniform jingled quietly from all the medals, and the leather strap of his worn sword belt creaked a little when he rested his hand on the hilt. The hilt was worn, too. He was like nobody else at court, wearing used things in the throne room, where everybody looked shiny all the time. Stisele herself looked shiny in embroidered satins, except for the big dirty streak. "You rolled in the mud, Stisele?"

"I'll show them," she said. She couldn't help it, she was shaking with anger again, just thinking about Jrene. "I'm a pirate, too."

Over in the corner, Flash and Blur fluttered with worry, and Blur drifted over to buzz in Stisele's ear. *Do not remind him,* she said.

As if anyone ever forgot.

"Emnir, your assessment?" said the moustache man.

"Right in front of her, Trebin?"

"Yes."

Emnir of Gorsae said, "I've seen her take on children two, three years older than herself, some much bigger, sometimes five of them at a time. Jrene's three years older, and the two of them get into a tussle at least once a week. Nothing deters Stisele, not even certain defeat. Her limbs are sound and straight, and she's strong for her age. She's a quick study. Her Royal Highness is clearly right, something can be made of the girl. But she has no respect for rank, and she'll never have any talent for weathercalling. I hesitate to set the precedent of taking her into the Order."

At that, Flash bounced frantically around the room. *Don't let them!* he buzzed. *Anything but the Order.* Stisele was a little bit afraid of the Order, too, though Emnir had always been kind to her.

Big Moustache Man—Trebin, that was what Emnir had called him—raised his eyebrows. "Her, into the Order?"

"But for her unfortunate parentage, I would have claimed her for training months ago."

Stisele began to suspect that Mommy Utroneth hadn't left her with these men for punishment after all. Months after her seventh birthday, nobody had yet decided how best to school her. It was past time.

Trebin shook his head. "Cutting the heir with her own weapon seems a poor prelude to a career in the Order. Especially for this one."

"Jrene started it," protested Stisele. "It's not fair."

"There's all the difference in the world between fairness and necessity," he said. He sounded like he really regretted saying so.

"I know." She looked down at her shoes. She'd torn the beadwork on the left one. Stupid shoe.

"Would you like to play Pirates and Commoners?"

That didn't make any sense. "With you?"

He laughed. It was a great big laugh that filled up the whole room, and right then Stisele decided she liked him. "I hadn't thought of that," he said. "Would you want to play Pirates and Commoners with me?"

"Only if I get to be the pirate."

"I'm awfully big."

"I'm fast. Emnir said so."

"Yes, he did," Trebin agreed. "But I'd had in mind that you would play with my daughter, if you don't mind my watching."

Stisele stood a little straighter. "She'll be the commoner, and I'll be the pirate?"

"If you like. She's a good sport."

"All right."

"Come with me, then." And he led her through the halls of the palace to the armory, where Stisele had never been allowed before. She could hear the place before she saw it—a constant clangor punctuated by barked commands and grunts of exertion poured into the hall from the practice courtyard. At the big doors, one of Mommy

Utroneth's uniformed young cousins shouted, "Colonel Trebin of Ythrae," to announce the moustached man. Inside the armory, various members of the House of Ambra let up their practice and turned to salute the Colonel with their weapons. A girl who had been sitting quietly on a chair much too big for her and polishing two wooden practice swords stood up and saluted Trebin with one of them. He called her over to him. "Harentil, bring them with you."

"Coming, Father." Harentil was bigger than Stisele, and maybe a year older. Her good court clothes were a lot less fancy than Stisele's. No mud, though, and Harentil looked like a proper child of the Crown Houses, with sleek, straight blonde hair and a square jaw.

The two girls sized each other up, and Stisele bristled at Harentil's frankly curious gaze. Harentil of Ythrae had never seen anyone like Stisele. Nobody ever had, because there was no one like Stisele. No one left living, anyway. "What?" Stisele demanded, though she knew what.

"Nothing," said Harentil, though it was everything.

"I get to be the pirate," Stisele announced, and watched to see what Harentil would make of that. The Ambra children usually laughed when she made a bid to play the winning side. All of them but Samren.

But Harentil cocked her head in thought. "Sure." She handed the practice swords to Stisele and said, "You pick."

They were nothing like the wooden knife Jrene had. These were light, almost springy, with no edge on them at all. It didn't matter which she chose, they were both the same, so she kept the one in her right hand and gave back the other.

Trebin looked around the armory, decided it was too crowded for children's games, however serious, and so led them out to the gardens. Flash and Blur faded into the sunlight. Stisele could still hear them buzzing apprehensively, following her through the hedge maze. It was too tall for her to see over, but Trebin seemed to know where they were going. Once he'd found them a suitable open space presided over by an apple tree in full white flower, he turned to the girls and said, "Ready?" They were. "Go."

Harentil loosened up her knees and just stood there waiting. This was going to be way too easy. Stisele charged at her, shrieking.

Maybe not so easy. When Stisele swung her sword at Harentil, the Ythrae girl slid past it and bonked her lightly on the head.

Stisele swung again, and Harentil ducked, then butted Stisele in the stomach with the hilt, hard enough to knock the breath out of her. "Oh!" said Harentil. "I'm sorry. I didn't mean to..."

But Stisele threw down her sword and ran to slam her body, full force, into her foe and knocked her clear over onto her back on the perfectly trimmed grass. "Surrender!"

she said, and swung her fists against Harentil. "Commoner filth!"

"That's enough," said Trebin.

"I said I was sorry," Harentil protested, trying to roll out from under Stisele's blows.

But Stisele had waited too long for her turn to be the pirate. She couldn't stop. "Yield the city!" she demanded. "Say it!"

Harentil struggled one last time to dislodge Stisele, who straddled her chest. "I will not."

"I said, that's enough." Trebin reached down to pick Stisele up by the back of her shirt and lifted her clear off of Harentil.

"The city is mine!" said Stisele as she hung from his grip like a kitten. She was crying now, crying and spitting, and what would Trebin think? She'd liked Trebin, and now nobody would ever teach her anything, and she'd be a useless bastard brat all her life. "It's my city, too." Whether she ever set foot there or not, it was one of the things she knew. Flash and Blur had been insistent on that point.

Harentil stood up and brushed broken blades of grass off her green-stained clothes. "Are you all right?" she asked Stisele.

Stisele knew to be ashamed of her dark hair, her loathing for Jrene, her temper, her bastardy, her dead commoner father, her dead slut mother, her cheekbones, her pointy chin, and her bad handwriting, but all of it together was nothing to the shame she felt, dangling

8

there by her shirt in mid-air above her unvanquished foe. "I'm fine," she said, though she couldn't stop crying. "You're not." Harentil's nose was bleeding all over her court satins. "I'm sorry."

Trebin sat on a marble bench and set Stisele back down on the grass. "Well, that was considerably more than I'd expected."

"You told me she'd fight dirty, Father," said Harentil. "It's my fault. I'd been warned."

"Come here," he said, and tended her nosebleed. "If it's anybody's fault, it's mine. Now. What did you learn from that match?"

Harentil sat next to her father on the bench. "People who aren't taught the rules of fencing don't follow them. It can be a kind of advantage."

They were talking about Stisele as if she weren't even there. Typical. "Can I be dismissed?" she said.

Trebin looked at her. "From now on, you don't ask for my dismissal. You wait for it."

But he didn't live in the palace. "Am I coming with you, then?" It was a dizzying thought. Leave Ambra Islet? What would Mommy Utroneth say?

"No," said Trebin. "Not yet. But I'll leave instructions for your training with the chief of the armory, and if you do as you're told, maybe later. Do you like horses?"

"I never saw one."

Trebin blinked. "Never saw one?"

"Samren wants one for his birthday, but Mommy Utroneth won't let them on the Islet."

Harentil looked at her father. "Mommy Utroneth?"

"You can't very well call the Sovereign Princess of Beltresa that in the city, Stisele."

Stisele's heart beat fast. *In* the city. In it. She'd been born on the Islet, and everybody knew she was never going to leave it. Anytime Jrene came home from her lessons in the realm she was to inherit, she'd boast of her travels to Stisele. When Stisele tried to correct Jrene on obvious errors of fact, things their tutors had been drumming into their heads as long as they'd been learning letters and numbers, the royal heir would say, *But how would you know? You'll never see it.*

Stisele said, "I can't go." Maybe nobody had told him. "Will you do as you're told?"

"Are you going to tell Mommy Utroneth?"

He blinked again at the name. "Of course. Will you do as you're told?"

"Yes."

"Do as you're told, Stisele, and you can hope to see the world, and please Her Royal Highness well, too."

At that, Stisele picked up her dropped weapon and saluted Trebin in showy imitation of Emnir. She felt her smile stretch far beyond the limits her nurse called dignified. "We live to serve."

"We do, indeed. You will report to the armory first thing in the morning. Your tutors will see to it. Now," he said, rising from the marble bench, "to inform Her Royal Highness. She wishes us to discuss the matter privately."

Flash and Blur were bouncing around among the apple blossoms overhead.

"Can I stay in the maze?" Stisele asked Trebin. "Just to think a little bit?"

Harentil turned her curious dark eyes back to Stisele and said nothing.

"You have plenty of new things to think about," said Trebin. "Get your thinking out of the way. Tomorrow, you'll have to start obeying. Dismissed."

"It was lovely to meet you," said Harentil, and that was when Stisele knew she'd been entirely bested.

"You can be the pirate next time."

Harentil shrugged, and her father took her hand and led her away.

Stisele watched them go, then climbed into the apple tree to catch up with Flash and Blur. "I'm going to see horses," she declared.

Blur, who languidly suffused the crown of the tree, said, *Trebin's all right. At least he's not in the Order.*

Flash bobbed about in circles around Stisele where she perched in the wye of the trunk. *Horses, nothing. You'll get to see the city. Come on.* He hopped up to the crown of the tree and brightened around Blur's faint edges. *Well? Come on!*

So Stisele climbed to the highest big branch she thought could hold her weight, where she could pop her head up out of the dome of blossoms. Such a perfectly happy smell. From here, she could see over the hedge maze and across the water to the city's many islands, where the spires of Beltresa's Guild Halls and the cupolae of the Crown Houses' palaces rose above the Sea of Oë. The early afternoon sun silvered the waves around Beltresa proper, and a few regulation clouds, under the management of the Royal Weather Agency, watered the mainland orchards of the Upriver Protectorate. The House of Ambra's tutors had taught her place names by pointing to shapes on maps. Sometimes she'd been allowed onto boats, when Jrene and Samren were getting lessons. Stisele's foster brother, who was almost a year older, had taught her some names while he pointed across the water: Point Quay, Morningside, Laddercrew Bridge, Southedge, and the tower at Calnir's Palace, which had been the seat of rule until Mommy Utroneth took over. From here, the spires all looked the same, and the bells all rang at once—even on Ambra Islet, Stisele could hear them ringing the hours, if the wind was favorable.

They rang second hour now. Today's lessons would be letting out in the nursery—the lessons she'd missed because she'd been bad. Stisele didn't like missing lessons. If Jrene and Samren got lots more of them than Stisele did, then lessons must be really good, so she loved the ones she got and stole others when she could. "What do you think they talked about without me?"

she asked Flash and Blur. Sometimes they knew things like that.

Flash bounded out of the tree, bounced around the hedges, and was back in an instant. *Ask Samren. He's looking for you.*

"Hey!" she called. "Samren!"

"Where are you?" His voice came faintly from somewhere over by the fountain, three loops of hedge passage away.

"Apple tree!" she hollered back.

A few moments later, he crawled under the foliage between two yew bushes. "Aha!" He scrambled up the apple tree, and Blur drifted aside so he wouldn't touch her. Flash and Blur didn't like touching anybody but Stisele.

"What did I miss?"

He brushed the garden dirt off his knees. "Accomplishments of the House of Imlen.."

She gripped her branch hard. "While I was gone?" It was so unfair.

"Because you were gone, they said. Your old cousin however-many-times-removed did some big things when he was Prince. Tutor says Mother would never have had to take over if Mocred of Imlen hadn't died in battle."

"Big things?"

"As big as all Upriver."

"Is Jrene still mad?"

"She's been waving her bandaged hand around, calling you a traitor. What did Mother do?"

13

"She got me a new teacher, and I'm going to the city, and I'll see horses, and Trebin of Ythrae says I'll get to see the world."

Samren looked wounded. "You don't have to lie about it."

"But she *did!*"

"Trebin of Ythrae? Who's he, anyway?" Samren remembered the dead people in the seven Crown Houses' genealogies well enough, but there were so many more living ones to keep track of. "He's not one of Ythrae's House elders, and nobody says he should be Prince instead of Mother."

"I don't know. He's got medals. And he let me be the pirate."

Samren looked skeptical about the whole thing. "Why would Mother do that?"

"Don't know. But I might get to ride a real horse."

"I got some bread." He pulled a crumbly slice of raisin loaf out of his pocket.

"Can I have some?"

He handed her the whole thing. "It's for you, silly. For stabbing Jrene."

"It wasn't that hard."

"Yeah, but I never get to stab Jrene."

Flash raced up the trunk of the tree to hover by Stisele's shoulder. *Utroneth's coming.*

So Stisele changed the subject. Mommy Utroneth wouldn't like the way Samren talked about stabbing his sister. Come to think of it, she might not like them talking about the House of Imlen's accomplishments, either. Stisele of Imlen wasn't supposed to know about certain things, or think about certain things—she definitely wasn't supposed to talk out loud about certain things. Sometimes it was stuff that should have been obvious to her, like asking which House would take the Crown from Ambra like Mommy Utroneth had taken it from Imlen. Sometimes it was weird stuff, like important kin-curses in history. Without Flash and Blur looking out for her, she'd have been in trouble all the time. "Do you think you'll get a horse for your birthday?"

Samren shook his head. "A boat, probably. I'm supposed to want to join the Fleet. Mother's talking about starting a school for it and sending me there as an example."

It was the first Stisele had heard about it. "But you won't go? Will you?"

"Mother gave me the speech again about how I'm supposed to be good at something and be all useful to Jrene when I grow up. Only I'm not good at anything. Serves Jrene right."

Stisele looked down from the tree, then whispered, "Your mother's almost here."

"We live to serve," said Samren, a little too loud.

Stisele giggled.

Below them, Utroneth, Fifth Sovereign of the Principality of Beltresa, peered up into the flowers and foliage. Flash and Blur hid behind Stisele.

Mommy Utroneth considered the sight of her son and her adopted daughter covered with crumbs in an apple tree. "Samren," she said.

"I didn't do it."

The golden circlet rose with her eyebrows. "Do what?"

"Whatever it is. It was probably Jrene."

"Come down from there, Samren."

He scrambled down the tree. "I have to go to next lesson," he said.

"Early? Your sailing master may die of shock."

"May I be dismissed?"

Mommy Utroneth sighed. "Yes, my darling. You may be dismissed."

He ran from the tree, scrabbled under the entangled branches of yew, and was gone through the maze.

The Sovereign Princess of Beltresa hitched her robes of royal red up just a little and sat in the tree's lowest wye. "It is a hard thing, Stisele, to be feared by one's children."

"I'm not afraid of you, Mommy Utroneth," said Stisele, and she climbed down to keep her adoptive mother company. Flash and Blur fluttered behind her, but she ignored them. What had Mommy Utroneth ever done to them?

"Did Samren tell *you* what he'd done? What he's so afraid I'll catch him at? Today, of all days, everyone can see how forgiving I am."

"He just brought me some bread, is all. He thought I was in trouble."

Mommy Utroneth smiled. "But instead, we have at long last figured out what to do with you. I knew we would. Anyone else would have had you killed when you were a baby."

"And some people still would." Stisele knew how Mommy Utroneth liked to see her kindnesses remembered.

"Many, many. But I knew, Stisele, that you would grow up to have a purpose. Long have I considered what that purpose ought best to be, and now I see it laid out before you. Will you show everyone that you're from good pirate stock, no matter what they say?"

"I will."

"Will you lay my enemies low?"

Stisele was so proud to be asked. "I'm not afraid of anybody."

"There are those who have called that a problem, but you and I know better, don't we?"

"Uh-huh."

"There is no act more virtuous than to repay trust with trust."

"I'm virtuous!"

"Yes, you are. Now, I'm trusting you to be obedient, no matter what the armory master tells you to do, no matter what Trebin tells you to do."

Stisele knit her brows. "What are they going to tell me to do?"

"In particular? I don't know. I'm trusting them, just like I'm trusting you. In general, though, they'll be making a mighty weapon of you."

Stisele knew this part, too. "Because there's no better weapon than the right person in the right place."

Utroneth was so pleased, she kissed Stisele on the forehead. "A mighty weapon in the service of the Crown. Now, you prove me right. Everybody will be watching."

Everybody always was. "I'll make you proud."

"Just one more thing, then."

"Anything."

"Don't cut Jrene again." She wagged her finger in the air between them, an amused smile on her lips. "No cutting the heir. Got it?"

"Got it!"

"For some time, I will be away," said Mommy Utroneth. "The Protectorate requires my attention. When I return from Twenty Locks, though, I expect to hear great things about your progress. I will be thinking of you, my dear."

"You're leaving?"

"Not for too long." And the Sovereign Princess of Beltresa permitted her adopted daughter to hang about her neck and kiss her on the cheek. After a moment, Utroneth adjusted the gold circlet over her slightly mussed golden hair. She stood, smoothed her red robes, and left Stisele in the maze.

When Utroneth had gone, Blur drooped about on the grass, and Flash rolled listlessly along the hedgetop. They were sullen all afternoon, and Stisele knew better than to bother asking why. Instead, she played Pirates all by herself, commanding the good ship *Marble Bench* to beset the beautiful city of Appletree, whose absolute submission she demanded, though after an hour of the tree's steadfast resistance, she accepted a conditional surrender. When the sky began to pink, she trailed one hand along the hedge and made her way back to the palace.

She was not the first to get back to the nursery for dinner. Clevi of Ambra, elderly nurse to the three royal children, was fussing over Samren and barely noticed Stisele's return.

"I'm fine," Samren protested.

"What happened?" asked Stisele. "Did Jrene stab you?"

Jrene stuck her tongue out at Stisele. "He fell in the drink. Again. Samren, I hope Mother puts you into the Fleet to drown. It'll serve you right."

Clevi said, "The Fleet will be your good right hand, one day. Are you wise to disparage it?"

"No," said Jrene, slouching in her chair.

"And your brother will be your good left hand, one day. It's not wise to disparage him, either."

"I'll disparage who I want."

"Whom," Clevi corrected her, and finally she noticed Stisele's clothes. "You can't eat dinner like that!"

Stisele had forgotten all about the grass stains. And the mud. And everything. "I'm sorry."

"Your shoe!"

"I didn't mean to."

Jrene sat up straight in her chair. "That's what happens when you dress commoners in silk."

Hands on her hips, Clevi turned to the eldest of her charges. "Jrene..."

"So if the Fleet's my right hand, and my brother's my left hand, what does that make Stisele? I know! She can be my..."

"Don't you say it out loud, child."

Blur, who had curled up under the table, stirred. *Oh, say it,* she muttered. *Go on, brat. Try me.*

But Stisele didn't like what Blur could do when she was angry. "Don't," she said.

"Are you trying to give me an order?" Jrene demanded.

Stisele swallowed her bitterness. "Please don't." Mommy Utroneth had been so mad last time it happened, and never again could Stisele blame anything on Blur. Nobody believed her about it.

That little bit of obeisance appeased Jrene, and Clevi got Stisele cleaned up and into a new suit of clothes before the bells across the water rang seventh hour. Then Clevi permitted the servants to enter with dinner.

The servants did not speak. They never spoke in Stisele's presence. They never glanced at her, though she stared at them, with their pale blue eyes and their sharp faces, all cheekbone and chin. Her father must have looked like that—they all looked alike. Ugly like Stisele was, only uglier.

In the morning, when Clevi set out Stisele's clothes, they weren't satins or muslins. Instead, Clevi presented her with rough canvas hand-me-downs that, as far as Stisele could tell, might have belonged to some commoner child.

"What is the meaning of this?" Stisele demanded.

"Well, don't we sound just like Her Royal Highness this morning?" Unperturbed, Clevi handed Stisele a pair of very new boots. These, at least, had been made for her. "The palace cobbler was up all night putting these together. I doubt you'll make short work of your shoes this time."

Stisele dismissed all thought of the palace cobbler and examined the boots. "Can I get mud on these?"

"Oh, I think that's inevitable."

"What's 'inevitable?'"

"Can't be avoided. Like summer heat and winter cold and the deaths of your parents."

"Inevitable," said Stisele, and ran her fingertips over the clothes she was allowed to get mud on. They even *felt* more purposeful than her court clothes.

Clevi said, "When you dress for your new training, you're to dress yourself from now on. I'll only help you with the formal things." Stisele would have whined about it, but Clevi added, "Unless, of course, you fail your new teachers." And then she left the room.

"Well, how do you like that?" Stisele asked Flash and Blur, once Clevi had gone.

Actually... said Blur.

Flash bounced over to pick up where Blur left off. *What we need to tell you is...*

We can't help you with this part, either. Blur drifted over the boots to consider them. *We'll be waiting for you here tonight. You'd never forgive us later, if we meddled with the day. And I don't think I can watch without meddling.*

"What are they going to do to me?" It occurred to Stisele that she ought to be afraid.

Make you a good soldier, said Flash.

"That's not so bad, then."

But they didn't answer. They just curled up on the foot of the bed together, Flash tucked into the center of Blur's warm nimbus, and for all Stisele knew, they might be asleep. If they slept. She'd never been sure.

Once she'd dressed, she braided her hair all by herself. She had to look in the mirror to do it. There was the ugly little girl with the pointy chin and the pointy cheekbones and the pointy nose and the dark hair with its impossible spirals that Clevi complained about every day. Now braiding it was Stisele's task to complain about. She grumbled through it, just like Clevi always had. Grumbling took the sting out of having to do it alone, having to do it at all, having to look at the ugly little girl in the mirror. Only the eyes were right, and even they looked wrong where they were, brave pirate brown in that commoner's face.

At breakfast, Samren looked with envy on Stisele's new boots. "I bet you get to kick stuff in those."

"They're proper pirate boots," said Stisele.

At breakfast, Samren looked with envy on Stisele's new boots. "I bet you get to kick stuff in those."

"Shows what you know," said Jrene. "You'd sink to the bottom of the sea in those things. They're soldier boots, like the Upriver Militia has. I saw them on the parade ground on Calnir's Prize. But you wouldn't know. You'll never see Calnir's Prize."

"Will too."

By eighth hour of the morning, Stisele reported to the armory chief. He knew who Stisele was—everyone did—but she'd never met him before. Govril of Ambra was uncommonly tall, and he bent himself in half to look Stisele in the eye. "I hear you're fearless."

Did people say so when she wasn't around? She flushed with pride. "It's true."

"You'll be fearless again someday. For now, say goodbye to it."

"But I..."

"Never contradict your instructions!" he barked into her face, and the sudden change in his voice, and the sense that she was shrinking as he straightened up to tower over her startled Stisele half out of her skin.

It seemed she had just said goodbye to her fearlessness.

Govril spent the morning ordering Stisele to run laps, climb rope ladders, lift staves, and stand still for what seemed like forever, shouting reminders to address him as *sir* whenever she forgot. Her nose itched terribly while she was supposed to be standing still, but she thought of what Jrene had said—*You'll never see Calnir's Prize. Will too.*

By lunch, she hurt all over. No other arrangements had been made for her, so Govril sent her back to Clevi to be fed. At the nursery table, Stisele was too hungry and tired to rise to any of Jrene's jibes or Samren's questions. She barely remembered to ask Samren what she was missing in lessons. He tried to tell her about the first ever kin-curse among the Crown Houses, during Calnir's reign when everybody still thought it was something only commoners could do. It was a big curse, too, with an earthquake that had leveled the first attempt at building a royal palace. This was just the kind of story grown-ups didn't tell when Stisele was around, so she wanted to know. She really did. But her eyes kept closing on her, and so many half-started dreams drifted into Samren's telling, Stisele knew she wasn't hearing him right.

When Clevi called naptime for Jrene and Samren, Stisele asked, "Am I allowed to have a nap, too?" She always had been before, but anything might happen now.

Clevi smiled. "Already much improved. Yes, dear, today you are ordered to have a nap."

So Stisele went to her room. Flash and Blur weren't on the foot of her bed anymore. She wanted to look for them, but all she could do was lie down.

When she woke, she found that her toes had blistered up, and she winced her way back into the boots.

At the armory, Govril saw her limp right away. "No more running today," he said. "Follow me." He led her past the courtyard, where the big kids were sparring. They ignored her as she passed.

"Why aren't we stopping?" she asked.

All the big kids' heads swivelled around to look.

Govril turned to face them. "What are the permissible questions?"

Silence.

"Esgol, you may answer."

A gangly boy said, "We may respond to orders by asking how, where, when, what, and who, sir."

"And the forbidden question?"

Silence.

"Esgol, you may continue."

"Why, sir."

"Why," said Govril, "is for lessons, not for orders."

"Why is for lessons, not for orders," the big kids repeated in unison, and halfway through, Stisele figured she was supposed to join them in saying so.

"Any questions, Stisele?"

"No, sir." Her voice came out in a tiny squeak, and the big kids laughed. *Mortification* was a word she'd learned from Clevi just last week. This was mortification.

Govril said, "We'll try this again. Follow me." And this time, Stisele followed silently.

He led her to a room filled with weapons of all kinds, stacked or racked or hung on the walls, each in accordance with its type. There were bows that bent forward and bows that bent back, all slack with their strings loose. Arrows were separated by length into long, tall vases—they made Stisele think of vases, anyway—and each length was fletched in differently colored feathers. Swords that curved were in one rack, and swords that were straight in another, both sets graded by size. Halberds loomed by the door. Over the big hearth, a pair of battered pirate cutlasses from the wandering years before the Principality hung far above her reach.

"Sit," Govril said, and Stisele dropped to the floor on the spot to comply. "At the table, Stisele."

In the center of the room, there was a huge oak table, and Stisele climbed up onto the chair to sit. Her legs kicked in the air nearly a foot above the floor. Govril dropped a pile of dirty rags and a tin of foul-smelling paste on the table before her, then carefully set a dozen sheathed knives within her short arms' reach. "You will polish these," he said.

"I'm not a servant!"

"Are you refusing an order?"

She hated herself for trembling. *Will too see the world.* "No, sir."

"Recite the Crown Contract."

It was such a weird thing to be asked under the circumstances, she stumbled a little on the preamble, but once she got her pace, she could do it without thinking. All the terms of Beltresa's surrender to Calnir of Ythrae and his pirate fleet came tumbling from her mouth, word for word. It was a point of pride for her that she could do it better than Jrene could, despite being three years younger. Flash and Blur had helped her learn it, practicing with her when nobody was looking. Stisele began with the commoners' acknowledgement of the pirates' superior force, proceeded through the clauses on obedience and taxation, blushed with shame through the clause forbidding miscegenation, and understood Govril's purpose when she reached the weapons clause. "The people of Beltresa, herein the commons, shall bear no blade longer than the width of the palm, on pain of death, nor shall they carry bow nor arrow nor spear on pain of death. These weapons they may make upon commission of the Crown only, but never test, nor shall such weapons be made for sale to other persons or powers except by permission of the Crown. Such implements of work as might be used as weapons shall be permitted only in accordance with Guilded labor, each such tool to be licensed by its Guild to a named master." There were more clauses, but she paused. "Do you want me to go on?"

"That will do." He could not conceal that he was impressed. "Now let's see if you know what it means."

She made a guess. "Are the servants allowed to polish these?"

"Do servants make knives?"

"Some commoners do. Jrene says, in the Smithing Guild, they make them with tongs. Is it true, they glow when they're hot?"

"Do *servants* make knives, Stisele?"

"No, sir."

"Then it is not for them to touch knives, except in the kitchen, under license by the Servants' Association. Her Royal Highness has decreed that the weapons clause does not apply to you. Your mother's blood outweighs your father's, so you will be permitted to touch these knives. And in time, if you do well, all the weapons in this room. Do you know how to polish a weapon?"

"No, sir. I never polished anything before."

He showed her, very slowly, what she needed to do. After all the barking, his patience over the rags and unguents bewildered her, but she tried not to let on. If she reminded him to start barking, he might not stop again. After a while, he left her by herself to finish. Alone with the knives, she was free to run her fingertips along them and think.

They knew what they were for, these knives did. There was a shining layer of purpose to them, and when she held one, Stisele thought about how she'd seen Jrene grip her wooden practice blade—a very particular sort of grip. She tried to hold the knife like that, but her hand was too small to get it right. Still, holding it made her feel purposeful, like she was *for* something. She'd be Mommy Utroneth's weapon.

Stisele knew not to spend too long listening through her hands. Nobody had any patience for it but her imaginary friends. Blur always sounded sad when she said no aristocrat would understand what Stisele's hands told her. Sometimes Flash would talk Stisele through it so she could find out more from the things she touched, but she didn't know if she'd ever get him to come with her into this room.

At the end of the day, Govril came to assess her work. Although she'd nicked herself up a bit, the blades were satisfactory.

"What is 'satisfactory?'"

"Good enough."

Stisele was good enough. Somebody other than Mommy Utroneth had said so. That evening in the nursery, none of Jrene's needling could touch her.

By then the blisters were so bad, Clevi allowed Stisele to go barefoot, even at the dinner table. Samren admired her blisters. "Real beauties," he said. "I got one on my thumb." He displayed it for everyone to see. "I went up the rigging today."

Jrene said, "Ew, don't wave that over the food."

"You're just jealous, Jrene."

Jrene stuck out her tongue. "I got to see the water-works this afternoon. They let me be watercaller. I didn't even have to touch the pipes to call it."

"Liar," said Samren. "Everybody has to touch the pipes."

"Everybody but Stisele," said Jrene, "because she'll never be able to call anything, anyway. What's she ever going to amount to on the battlefield? She can't even call the weather."

"I can, too." But they all knew she couldn't.

"That's enough," said Clevi. "Stisele worked hard today."

"What did I miss in morning lessons?"

Samren looked abashed. "Weathercalling. Boring principles. You'd have hated it."

Jrene said, "We get to do all the good stuff, now that you're gone. And what did you do today?"

"I polished fighting knives." Stisele sat a little straighter. "Like a servant!"

So Stisele recited the weapons clause perfectly, the whole thing, just because she could. "Shows what *you* know, Jrene."

Jrene stood from the table and stomped out of the room, slamming her bedroom door behind her.

"What?" Stisele said.

Samren said, "She couldn't even get through the preamble for Tutor this morning."

So he and Stisele drilled each other through the whole thing, hoping Jrene would come back in the middle and hear how well they could do it. Clevi sat at the table with one finger pressed to the center of her forehead as if with a piercing headache, saying nothing.

But Jrene didn't come back. Stisele stumbled to bed early on her blistered feet, and barely kept awake to tell Flash and Blur how her day had gone. They buzzed their familiar lullaby buzz, and she fell asleep to one of Flash's tales of talking animals.

The next day was much the same, but less embarrassing. It was easy to call Govril sir, because he knew things she didn't. It was hard to run in the boots, which Stisele was coming to hate, but she ran when he told her to run, she climbed whatever he told her to climb, and she stole glances at what he had the big kids doing whenever she was between orders. She liked polishing the cavalry sabers even more than she'd liked the knives. When Govril sat with her to show her how, she said, "Is this a lesson, sir?"

"You can ask questions now, yes." Govril was so still and calm, cleaning the sword he took up for his example, he hardly seemed the same man who did all that barking.

Some of the sabers were straight and some were curvy. Some were sharp on both sides, and some on only one. To her hands, all of them were about speed and strength. There were differences, but she couldn't tell what they meant. "If they're all for when you ride a horse, how come they're different from each other?"

"Well, there's heavy cavalry, and there's light cavalry. I bet you can see which swords are for which."

"Uh-huh."

He pulled a little sack of toy wooden soldiers from a cabinet and poured them out over the table. While he set the footsoldiers up in lines, his smile was so like Samren's.

The cavalrymen Govril clustered together to face the line of footsoldiers. "The hussars in the heavy cavalry go like this, in little bunches, and they charge into the enemy line as hard as they can, to break it wide open in one place. You go ahead."

Stisele cupped her hands around the wedge of cavalrymen and banged them into the line. Footsoldiers flew everywhere, and she laughed while she picked them up off the floor.

Govril laughed, too, while he set the line back up. "But the light cavalry, they do a couple of things. The uhlans ride back and forth in front of the enemy lines and shoot them with arrows, to break the line in a lot of little places." He nodded his permission to her.

The wooden horsewoman in her hand sped across the table, and Stisele alternated battle cries with her best attempt at the twang of a bowstring. Every time she twanged, Govril knocked over a footsoldier and said, "Oof!"

When Stisele had had enough of that, she asked, "What's the other thing?"

"The other thing? Oh, the other thing light cavalry does. Scouting, reconnaissance. The dragoons in the light cavalry go around when you're between one big battle and the next, and they harry the enemy and then run back with news." Govril set the footsoldiers up into a circle and picked one up to make it say, "It's a good thing we're camped safely here, far away from those wicked Beltresins."

The wooden horsewoman in her hand sped across the table, and Stisele alternated battle cries with her best attempt at the twang of a bowstring.

"No, you're not!" Stisele said, and her handful of dragoons galloped by and twanged their bowstrings at the footsoldiers, who yelped and fell over, one by one.

"They all do other things, too, of course," Govril said as he swept a hand across the table to tumble the soldiers back into their sack. "But that's enough for today, *if* you remember it." So he quizzed her a little on hussars, uhlans, and dragoons, until she could stop laughing at their funny names, and then she got to guess which sabers did what.

She could barely pick up the straight double-edged sabers of the hussars, even using both hands. "Is this the same kind Trebin of Ythrae has?"

"Trebin of Ythrae has a great many weapons. Why do you ask?"

"The one he was wearing was shaped like this. I think. Sir."

"You have a good eye. Good memory, too."

"Who is he?"

"He's the best cavalry officer in his House's troop levy. Just like your mother does, he wants one army for Beltresa and one fleet, with all the Houses mixed up together. No more separate House levies with separate chains of command. It's a hard thing to push for."

Stisele scrunched her eyebrows together to remember the lessons she used to have with Samren and Jrene. Used to have—strange to think they were over now. "Like the Order and the Weather Agency got squashed together."

"Just like them, when your cousin Mocred was Prince. It's a pity and a shame the Efa navy killed him, as Her Royal Highness always says. All the city's defenses ought to report directly to the Princess, if we're going to keep the Efa out. The more the other Houses see the House of Ythrae cast its lot with us in Ambra, the more they'll all fall in line. Even Imlen. We don't always get along, but none of us would do better if the Emperor of Efa took over. Your Imlen kin know that, I think. They're not fools."

He didn't sound altogether sure of Stisele's Imlen kin. But she didn't really know any of them, so she kept her mouth shut. Mommy Utroneth said a royal weapon like

Stisele must be sheathed in royalty — she'd be useless for managing her Imlen kin if she lived with them.

Govril only left Stisele alone a short while that afternoon. Long enough, though, for her to get a feel for the sabers' sense of purpose. The saber she liked best was about swiftness above all. So maybe Trebin was about swiftness, too.

Things were about other things, that was what her hands told her.

That evening, all her bickering with Jrene was lackluster, and Samren soon gave up on Stisele to go play with his wooden ships. Flash and Blur waited in Stisele's bedroom, but she went straight to sleep without more than hello.

On the third day at the armory, Stisele found she was numb through and through once her day's training was done. Jrene seemed to be talking from very far away, and it didn't much matter what she said. Stisele had a vague sense of missing Samren and Clevi, which was odd, because they were right there at dinner with her when she noticed it. That night, Flash and Blur leaned up next to her while she slept, like they would when she got sick. She wished they wouldn't. She wasn't sick, she mustn't get sick, or she'd never get to see the world. But she was too tired to say so. There they stayed, nestled in the crook of her neck.

In the morning, she couldn't get her boots on at all. Clevi came in to see what was keeping her from breakfast, and found Stisele weeping over the bloody mess of her feet. Flash and Blur were so agitated, Stisele couldn't make sense of them for the buzzing.

"Oh!" said Clevi. "Stop that, dear. It's not going to work."

"My socks are too small."

"I'm sending for the physician."

Stisele wailed.

"Surely you want him to make your feet stop hurting."

"I want the armory. I want to see Calnir's Prize. Mommy Utroneth will be so mad."

"She'd be mad at me if she saw your feet and I hadn't sent for the physician. You get right back into bed."

"But, Clevi!"

"Right now, young lady."

While Clevi was out, Samren snuck into the room with a biscuit from the breakfast table, and Stisele got crumbs all over her sheets. "What happened to your feet?" he asked.

"Don't know."

"They smell."

"So do yours."

"I got another biscuit in my pocket."

"Gimme." She was so hungry, she couldn't stop, even though she felt queasy.

Clevi returned with the court physician before Stisele managed to finish the second biscuit. She crammed the remaining three bites' worth into her mouth and so could not answer when Nethrenilorhem said, "I see your appetite is not adversely affected." Stisele liked Nethrenilorhem's Jhislaini accent and the way he used big words with her just as if she were a grown-up. He was kind of funny looking, with his young face and his hair already gray. There weren't many foreigners Mommy Utroneth trusted, but Nethrenilorhem could be told anything.

"I hurt my feet," Stisele said, spilling more crumbs on her bed.

"You certainly did. Will you be brave for me?" He waited for her to nod her head before he gently pulled off the bloody socks. He gripped her right leg at mid-calf with one of his big hands and examined the foot from all angles. "Blossoming infection you've got there. Why didn't you say anything sooner?"

"Nobody asked."

Now the left leg. "It didn't occur to you to say you wanted a day off?"

"I'm going to see the world. And Mommy Utroneth needs a weapon."

"Both true, no doubt. But you won't be much of a weapon in your current state."

"But I have to go to the armory!"

"Govril's already been informed. Physicians get to give orders, too, you know."

"Yes, sir," Stisele answered reflexively.

That took him aback. "You're a quick study."

"I'm going to see the world."

"I pity anyone who tries to stop you. Just, one thing at a time."

Two servants carried in a basin of warm water, into which Nethrenilorhem stirred a dull greenish powder. He had her sit at the edge of the bed while he cleaned her blisters. All the while, Flash and Blur bobbed in circles around the room. Stisele would have said they were pacing, if anyone had been willing to believe her about them. The water was nice, and the powder was doing whatever it was supposed to, but Nethrenilorhem used a cotton cloth to rub her blisters. Light as his touch was, it was still so sharp, she couldn't help crying. She knew, if she could just make it to the end of the washing, he might carry her pain for her, but it was hard.

The room was too crowded, with Clevi and Samren and the physician all clustered around her, and the servants watching. Stisele hated that servants were watching her cry. "Make them go away," she said.

"I'm working on it," Nethrenilorhem assured her.

"Not them. Them!" She pointed at the servants, who did not flinch.

Flash said, *That's not nice, love.*

"I don't care if it's not nice!"

Clevi cocked her head in puzzlement, but turned to dismiss the servants nonetheless.

No sooner had they gone than Jrene came to see what the fuss was about. "Oh, did the little baby scuff herself?"

SARAH AVERY

That's it, said Blur, and she started trying to climb into Stisele's mouth. *I've had it. Let me at her. Come on, just once, say something really good.*

Darling, Flash said, *that's a very bad idea.*

"I don't care," said Stisele. She felt like she was boiling inside, like she'd swallowed Blur altogether, and she hated Jrene, hated her hated her hated her.

"Well, you sound like you care," said Jrene. "You sound like it, from in the nursery, and from out in the hall, and Tutor in the library can hear you sound like you care, and I bet all the big kids in the armory can hear it, too. Listen to you cry cry cry." And the heir to the rule of Beltresa screwed up her eyes and let out a piercing imitation of human misery.

Nethrenilorhem did not turn to look. "Clevi, would you be so kind as to escort the heir from the room before..."

Trip and fall, Blur suggested from somewhere behind Stisele's sternum. *That's a good one.*

Clevi was already on it. She set her hands on Jrene's shoulders and was gently turning her to direct her back out of the room. Jrene was too busy scrunching her face up in mockery of her foster sister to pay any attention.

"Trip and fall," said Stisele, and Blur launched herself from Stisele's mouth to fly, bright, through the air and barrel into Jrene's back. The whole room shivered, and the water in the basin splashed onto the carpet by Stisele's bedside.

Jrene went sprawling face first onto the tiles, then stood up bleeding from scrapes on her knees and forehead, crying in earnest now and pointing an accusatory finger at Stisele. "She kin-cursed me!"

Samren was, for once, unimpressed. "Oh, like you don't try to do it to her, every chance you get."

"It was only a matter of time," said Clevi.

Nethrenilorhem was finally done bathing Stisele's feet. "All right, Jrene. I'll be with you in your room in a moment." Jrene went, wailing like a fire claxon. The physician stood from the floor where he'd knelt, and smoothed his robes. "Well, that makes, what, two months since last time?"

"About that," Clevi agreed.

Stisele didn't like the way this was going. "Last time, she did it to me!"

"Last time," Clevi reminded her, "you snuck into her room to cut her hair while she slept. She was entirely justified."

"So was I."

No, really, said Flash, *you weren't.*

"But I was!"

Besides, we told you not to, that time, Blur added.

"There's nothing for it," said Clevi. "We'll have to mention this to Her Royal Highness."

"No!"

"Think about what you've done, Stisele," said Nethrenilorhem, and he left without even offering to carry the blister pain. He wasn't obligated to burden his body like that for just any old thing, and she knew it, but she'd hoped.

Samren said, "Jrene was asking for it."

"Yes," said Clevi, "but if we all got everything we asked for, we'd all be in big trouble all the time, wouldn't we?" It was so hard to argue with her. She shooed Samren into the nursery, and though he looked back at Stisele, he didn't resist.

Nethrenilorhem closed the door, and Stisele was alone with her imaginary friends.

Flash said, *I told you it was a bad idea.*

She really was *asking for it,* Blur insisted.

"She was," Stisele agreed, though she wished she hadn't given in.

Stay here, said Flash, and he squeezed under the bedroom door and out.

Blur warmed the bedclothes back up. *You might as well lie down. I doubt you're going anywhere today.*

Stisele lay down on the bed and didn't object when Blur settled in to stroke her hair. "It's not fair."

So few things are. You've been a brave little soldier these past few days. Do you like it?

"I'm going to be the best soldier in Mommy Utroneth's whole cavalry."

Flash popped back in under the door and said, *Yes, but do you* like *it?*

Stisele was afraid she would cry again. "What if they don't let me go back?"

Oh, I don't think you have to worry about that, said Flash, though he sounded worried about something, himself.

Why not? Blur asked.

Stisele, how would you feel if they moved you into a room far away from Jrene?

"I hate Jrene."

Of course you do, said Blur. *But far away from Jrene might be far away from Samren and Clevi.*

"Oh." That didn't sound so good. "Can't they come with me? Or Jrene could leave the nursery. She's always saying she's too big for it."

I don't know, said Flash. *Just be ready for the possibility.*

There was a knock at the door. "Coming in," said Nethrenilorhem's voice, and soon all the rest of him followed. He was stirring some kind of poultice in a bowl.

"Am I in trouble?"

"Less than on the day you were born."

"You always say that."

"Still true. Now, if I carry the pain for you, are you going to run all over the place on those bloody little feet?"

"No, sir."

"You don't have to call me sir."

"Well, I won't. Run all over the place."

"You'll stay in bed and rest and read for your lessons."

"I'm not getting lessons anymore. Not with books."

He frowned. "I see. I'll send you a book you'll like, if you stay in bed."

"All right."

"All day, in bed."

"Yes, sir."

"That settles it, then. Show me your feet." She did, and once he'd slathered her from calves to toes in the cooling poultice, he rested his big hands on her knees to draw the pain out. All her pain. The blisters had been so bad, she hadn't even noticed how much she hurt everywhere else. She breathed easy, and he slumped and caught his breath. "You would have gone back to the armory like this if we'd let you?"

"I'm going to..."

"See the world, yes." He stood to go, a bit unsteady on his feet. "It'll be an interesting day, carrying this. Remember your promise."

"I can take orders."

"Make sure you keep that up. When the Princess gets home from Twenty Locks next week, she'd better have good news to outweigh that curse." He picked up the offending boots. "I'll see what can be done about these."

It was such a relief to be without pain, Stisele fell asleep right away, and didn't wake up until Clevi came in carrying an enormous book. "Feeling better?"

"He took it all."

"He was kinder than you deserved."

Stisele didn't answer.

"Anyway, he sent you this. Are your hands clean?"

They weren't, so Clevi brought a damp cloth to wash them. All the while, Stisele gazed with longing at the book, just now out of reach on her footstool.

"Be careful with it, child. Send it back in one piece." And Clevi left her to play with it.

The cover of plain black leather bore no words, but inside, on the endpaper, someone had written in high scribal handwriting, *Last Works of Foril, A Master Printer of Beltresa. Twelfth Year of the Principality. 7/100.*

"Seven one-hundredths? What does that mean?"

Seventh copy of one hundred copies, Flash said. *That means it's really rare, and this one is especially good.*

"Foril." It was a commoner's name. Most masters in the Guilds were commoners. "Who wants to read a book by somebody named Foril?"

Blur shimmered with anticipation. *You don't read it. Just look.*

It was a volume of woodblock prints on soft, fat pages—landscapes and city scenes of famous places all over the world, so beautifully done that Stisele felt like she could just fall right into them. Between the heavy pages were sheets of delicate, translucent paper that showed the ghosts of the bold images. Her avid eyes took in the views of Beltresa she could not see from home. She pored over the great western market, Calnir's Square, and, strangest of all, Ambra Islet before

Mommy Utroneth's palace was built. Ambra Islet looked positively unnatural, with its black cliffs rising from the sea to a flat expanse of green pasture with nothing on it but some cows, a cowherd, and a shack for the cowherd to live in. Looking closely, Stisele could see the old stairs cut into the rock, and a tiny boat tied and bobbing at the bottom. As strange as it was to see what home had looked like before Mommy Utroneth moved the seat of rule, it was disorienting to look at home *from someplace else.*

The thought gave her shivers.

The book showed her the Upriver Protectorate's second city, Harbortown, sprawling around the mouth of the river Eboë, curved like a crescent moon around the islands of Beltresa. Stisele examined with particular curiosity the city of Twenty Locks, cut into the face of the Escarpment, with the River Eboë on one side and the famous twenty-stepped locks of the Upland Canal on the other. "Come home soon," she said to the figure standing on the tall bridge before the falls. "Come home, Mommy."

The printer had obviously taken liberties with the far-off desert cities of Too Long and Even Longer, and the Forest Wall in the north appeared to be made entirely of light and fog, but the Augurs' Hearths in Miaaro were rendered in obsessive detail, with their low domes and humble stone fences. The city of Efa rose in gleaming white marble from the shores of the ocean, where the inland seas of Oë and Jhislain poured out into the unknown. Stisele marveled for the first time at the majesty of Beltresa's adversary. How did anyone stand a chance against Efa?

The views of Jhislain were yellowed a little more than the other pages, and a scrap of paper with a list of medicinal plants held the place for the first of them. Jhislain was a city of gardens, famed for scent and spices and medicine. Its switchbacked streets were as much bloom as stone in Foril's images. Stisele read the caption on the most yellowed of the pages, "The College of Physicians and the College of Courtesans at High Flowering Festival." In the center of a crowded piazza between two sets of stone gates, a pair of sword dancers twirled.

"Do you suppose Nethrenilorhem gets homesick?" Stisele asked Flash and Blur.

He'd go home if he could, Blur said. *Where will you go, when you grow up?*

"All of them."

Flash rolled across the big page to look at some detail in the picture of High Flowering Festival. *It would be a very dire thing for the world if the best cavalry soldier in 'Utroneth's army went campaigning in all these places.*

"They'd never stand a chance," said Stisele, and she almost pitied them. "Except Efa. Efa looks really big. That would be a fair fight."

It'll be up to 'Utroneth, Flash reminded her. *And Jrene, someday.*

"Wherever Mommy Utroneth sends me," said Stisele. She didn't like to think about Jrene replacing the Princess. "We live to serve."

You just keep saying that, said Blur. *That's what will keep you alive.*

Right until the day they send her to war, Flash pointed out. He didn't sound at all happy about it.

One problem at a time, said Blur. *It can only help that she'll learn to defend herself.*

Flash didn't answer. He just bounced up to perch on Stisele's shoulder. *Let's look at the Guild Halls again.*

So she flipped back to the views of Beltresa. Each Guild Hall had its spire, its bells, its park. Stisele pretended to humor Flash; she wanted to see the seven palaces of the Crown Houses on the island of Calnir's Prize. She tried turning the pages one at a time, planning to linger over the ones she needed, but in Foril's day the palaces had all been construction sites in their first wave of building. Scaffolds and pulleys surrounded half-finished cupolae. Workmen whose only discernible features were their curly dark hair clambered up the open walls. Even the Royal Weather Agency's distinctive tower was nothing yet but an inscribed cornerstone, caught in the princely ceremony of its laying. So Stisele sought pages for things that would still look the same. Flash won out after all, and buzzed on and on about the glories of the commoners' Guilds, which he was sure would stand to the end of time, until she fell asleep.

Clevi brought Stisele her meals to eat alone in her room, and Samren did not come to see her, which meant someone was watching him. Merely forbidding him would not have been enough.

In the morning, Stisele woke up already sullen about having been left so much alone the day before, though when she washed the crust of poultice off her feet, she found they were much improved. She padded barefoot out for breakfast—Nethrenilorhem had not sent back the boots—and found that Jrene wasn't speaking to her. Fine. The two girls conspicuously ignored one another, trying to trade insults through Samren, who got sick of them both and left the table.

Clevi looked downright pale. "Girls. A long time ago, I had a sister. When we were little, we thought we hated each other."

"But I *do* hate her!" Jrene protested.

"And my sister and I said the same, at your age. Many times. But when we grew up, we became best friends. We'd never have believed it. Nobody was as surprised as we were, but that's what happened. I miss her so terribly. Now that she's gone, I would give anything to go back and start our friendship earlier, to have more days like the last ones."

Stisele said, "What happened to her?"

"She was ship's weathercaller on the *Ambra* when Prince Mocred drove the Efa Imperial Navy from the Sea of Oë. The weathercallers from the different House levies weren't working together, and when the House of Locrisse pulled the lightning that sank the Efa flagship, a forking branch of the lightning got my sister, too."

"Stupid Locrisse," said Jrene, by way of comfort.

"One Fleet," said Stisele. "That's why Mommy Utroneth says there has to be uniformication."

"Unification, dear. Yes. Now, say you'll make up with Jrene before you go back to the armory."

"I'm going back to the armory?"

"After you make up with your sister, yes."

Jrene narrowed her eyes. "So if I don't make up with her, she doesn't get to go?"

Clevi sighed. "If she can't go, you'll be stuck with her for lessons all day."

So the girls made up right away.

Stisele remembered. "I don't have my boots."

"You'll go in your slippers."

"My slippers! In the armory?" The big kids would all be looking.

"Govril understands."

But Stisele didn't. She sulked and knocked things over and braided her hair badly so Clevi had undo it for her and start again. "I want my boots back," Stisele said when Clevi tried to cajole her into her beaded slippers. The broken beadwork was all mended.

Clevi looked at Stisele's feet, still swollen red and covered with scabs. "You want your boots back. Goodness. Sorry, General. Can't be done."

General! Didn't that sound fine! "But I order you…"

"Here's some tactical advice from your old nurse: When can't meets must, can't wins."

"Huh?"

"When can't meets must, can't wins. Just practice to understand it. Believe me, one day you'll see what I mean."

Stisele repeated the words to herself all the way to the armory, over and over, until they were just sounds that meant so little they couldn't even confuse her anymore.

When Govril greeted her at the armory door, he demanded to see her feet. "Polishing today," he said, and put her to work with a pile of unstrung bows and a bottle of linseed oil.

"When do I get to do the halberds?"

"When you're about a foot taller."

So Stisele tried to think tall thoughts while she polished the bows.

Two more days passed before she got her boots back. When Nethrenilorhem returned them to her room, the leather was wrinkly, for all that they had a fresh polish on them. "The palace cobbler put some wear on them for you," said the physician. "If you were nicer to the servants, it might cross their minds to do that kind of thing before the fact."

"I'm not allowed to talk to servants." Everybody knew that.

"And yet you're able to be rude to them without addressing them directly. It's a remarkable skill. What if you tried being *polite* to them without addressing them directly? It wouldn't be any harder."

"Hmph." She'd heard that before. Flash had told her more or less the same thing, a bunch of times.

Stisele had imagined getting the boots back would mean more running and climbing and jumping, but instead, the next thing Govril had her do in the armory was learn to stand.

"But I know how to stand. Um, sir."

Govril bent in half to look her in the eye. "That's the problem. You have to unlearn what you've got."

"Why...I mean...how? Sir." She was so embarrassed at the ground she'd lost in her training, she could have wept, but he didn't bark at her this time.

He gave her stances and then made her hold them for half an hour at a stretch, with a few minutes to run around in between. Standing still was the hardest thing he'd made her do yet, but she wanted Mommy Utroneth to be proud when she came home.

The day the Princess returned from Twenty Locks was cloudless and warm, exactly as scheduled. As the royal barge scudded across the wavelets from the city, trumpets greeted Utroneth from Ambra Islet. Stisele was scrubbed clean and gussied up in white silk and lace. None of her protests to Clevi had softened the old nurse on the subject of Stisele's boots, which the girl had been certain would make the best possible impression on her mother. Instead, Stisele had to stand at the back of the carefully choreographed assembly that waited for the royal barge to land.

Jrene and Samren, though, *they* got to wait right at the dock's edge.

Holding Clevi's hand, Stisele watched her foster mother greet the heir, and then the spare. And then Utroneth glided up the carved stone stairs without a word to anyone else.

"Hey, Clevi," said Stisele.

Clevi sighed. "Yes, General?"

"Someone tattled, huh?"

"The best way to keep people from tattling is to give them nothing to tattle about. And yes, I tattled. Would you rather she'd heard it from Jrene?"

Stisele sulked her way up the stairs, kicked Clevi in the shin when they got up to the greensward, and ran off to the maze the moment the old nurse let go her hand. Her imaginary friends buzzed along behind her.

Blur said, *You really shouldn't have kicked Clevi.*

Besides, said Flash, *you don't even know what she told the Princess.*

At the top of the apple tree, it was easier to believe them. There, where white blossoms only now began to give way to dark leaves, Stisele nursed her sullenness a long time. She stared across the water at the city, making up stories to herself about all the things she would never be allowed to do, now that Mommy Utroneth was so mad she wouldn't even talk to her. Again.

The Princess's voice drifted over the yew hedge. Stisele perked up—if her mother was looking for her, then everything would be all right.

Flash sped up the tree trunk. *Hold still!* he said. *They don't know you're here.*

In the quietest whisper she could manage, Stisele said, "Then I'll tell them."

Hush, said Blur. *Stop squirming.*

So Stisele clung to the branch and listened.

Utroneth sat miserably on the marble bench. "The House elders would have me put her down. It has been a heavy enough burden to have killed one child to take the crown. After Mocred's heir...after Vesrelim...I had hoped I would never have to do it again. But when I measure one little life against the good of the Principality, I always get the same answer."

Emnir said, "If it must be done, I can make it painless. She won't have to know a moment of fear." His voice was heavy with regret.

"I'd owe her at least that," said Utroneth. "That, or to do it myself. Blast it, she deserves better than the least I would do for my horse. Really, what has she ever done that I wouldn't have? It might have been kinder to settle the matter the day she was born."

Trebin asked, "Is it decided, then?" Silence. "I would take her south with me, if it made any difference."

Emnir sounded skeptical. "A child of seven, underfoot while you're campaigning? And I feared Her Royal Highness and I had fallen prey to sentimentality."

"When our forebears were pirates, they thought nothing of going into battle with their children underfoot. And Stisele is uncommonly promising, as you yourselves first recognized."

"No," said Mommy Utroneth. "I haven't the heart to send her to war so soon."

"So you would kill her in her sleep at home, instead." There was no accusation in Trebin's voice, just a careful weighing of options. "Well, I've seen worse ways to die."

"The Order could still set her straight," suggested Emnir. "We could remove her to the Fortress for training. Fourteen years out of Jrene's sight, and she'd be a different person when they met again. The other recruits get home visits, but Stisele's accustomed to being the unfortunate exception."

"Not the Order," said Utroneth. "Training a half-commoner in assassination is not a precedent we can set. You were right, Emnir, to say so before. No." The Princess put her head in her hands. "Look at the respect and affection she calls out of us. Out of *us,* the usurper bitch and her hardened henchmen. If we could give her a good purpose, what might we not accomplish through her?

Even Govril has offered to take her in, young as she is."

Trebin said, "Is Govril's dormitory far enough away from your daughter?"

"I'm not sure anywhere on the Islet is far enough. If the girls had a few years apart, they might come to look back on all this with nostalgia. Stranger things happen."

"I have a daughter who never wanted to be an only child," said Trebin. "And I have a pack of House elders who would do almost anything to tweak the House of Imlen. They've resigned themselves to your reign, but they'll never forgive Mocred for poisoning Calnir's heirs."

"Never?"

"Not in this generation. Build your Fleet Academy, and after a hundred years of fighting common enemies together, maybe things will be different."

Mommy Utroneth stood from the marble bench. "If the ruler of your House tells me himself that he consents, Stisele will foster with you. I would not presume to dictate to House rulers who will live in their palaces."

"It will go better if you give him a week to dicker with the other elders. Let them persuade themselves it's their own idea. Can you keep her one more week?"

"If she can't refrain from throwing curses even for one week, then we have no choice but to put her down, whatever we ourselves would prefer. For the Crown's sake. And hers. The longer we wait to take some kind of action, the less my close-cousins will scruple about killing her and calling it patriotic service."

"Agreed," said Trebin. "I will do what I can."

"Trebin, I will not forget that you offered my daughter shelter when I could not."

"I will not forget that you hold her as your daughter."

"Go, then."

Stisele caught sight of his uniform through the branches as he left. He really was going to take her away. If he could.

And then, for the first time in her life, Stisele heard Mommy Utroneth crying. It was a small, angry sort of crying she did, carefully contained. Oh, to be able to cry like that, with dignity. Stisele made up her mind she would never wail again, never cry like a little baby who scuffed herself. Once the first moment of wonder had passed, Stisele wanted nothing but to climb down the tree and comfort the Princess.

Don't, said Blur. *Don't force her hand. See how much she wants you to live? Do not move.*

If Govril had not made her practice and practice at keeping still in the armory, she could never have got through it. Flash and Blur hovered under her as if they could hold her up, though bitter experience had proved they couldn't.

Stisele tried to think holding-still thoughts, tree thoughts. Part of her mind catalogued Mommy Utroneth's many close-cousins, trying to guess which ones would kill her, and how. Ridiculous. What could those lace and silk people do to a good soldier like Stisele?

And then, for the first time in her life, Stisele heard Mommy Utroneth
crying.

It was not long before Mommy Utroneth daubed
her eyes with her sleeve and slowly, one hesitant step
at a time, left the maze. Emnir of Gorsae followed her
without a word.

Wait here, Flash said, and he bounded off to follow
them.

Blur looked all frayed at the edges. *We must not curse*
them again.

Stisele whispered, "It wasn't my fault."

No. This time, it was all my doing. I can't even know
it won't happen again. You have no idea how hard this is.

"It's so unfair. You're not even real, and you made Mommy Utroneth cry."

Blur didn't contradict her.

After a few moments of awkward silence, Flash rushed back. *You can come down now, loves. They've gone in.*

Stisele climbed down, but she didn't talk to Flash or Blur all the way back through the maze, where they had privacy, or in the halls of the palace, where they didn't— though that hadn't always stopped Stisele before. In the nursery, she wasn't speaking to anybody. Samren held up one of his toy ships and invited her to be the Efa navy, and she just glared at him.

"All right, you can be the Beltresin fleet, and I'll be the Efa navy. You win."

She sat heavily down on the floor beside her brother and took the little carrack in her hand. And wept. She did it just like Mommy Utroneth did, all small and quiet and angry.

"What?"

"Will you always be my brother, no matter what?"

He looked so confused. "No matter what. We don't get to pick, or I wouldn't be stuck with Jrene, silly."

"I want to be Beltresa."

They had a battle for a while, but her heart wasn't in it. Samren begged off, saying he had to prepare for lessons tomorrow, so Stisele went to her room.

We'll think of something, said Flash.

"I'm not talking to you. You're imaginary."

Nobody answered.

"Do you hear me? I said, you're imaginary."

The silence went on far too long. What if they really were just imaginary? But Blur had picked a fight with Jrene. Blur had nearly got Stisele killed. Might get her killed yet.

Flash and Blur could be wrong. That was even scarier than their nonexistence.

Stisele grabbed the first thing she saw and threw it at the wall. A beaded slipper. The second thing she found was a pillow. It bounced off the leaded panes of her window. The third thing was Nethrenilorhem's book, and she couldn't throw that. Just couldn't.

"What am I going to do?"

No answer.

She searched the room for Flash and Blur, and found them under the bed, quivering. "What am I going to do?" she demanded.

We never know, said Blur. *You're wonderful that way.*

"I should go now."

Where? said Flash.

"Someplace somebody wants me. The armory. Govril wants me there."

Blur said, *You mustn't let them know you were spying.*

"*We* were spying."

Yes, we were, Blur admitted, *but spying only works if nobody catches you. If they catch you, they get to kill you.*

It sounded like a really bad variation on playing Pirates and Commoners. "You're always spying, all the time. Don't you get scared?"

We've got nothing to lose but you, said Flash. *But you have everything ahead of you.*

Almost everything, Blur added ruefully.

Flash stuck to the positive. *You're going to see the world.* Stisele tried packing the few things that were precious to her, but once she'd set them aside, she realized she had nothing to pack them in. Flash and Blur eventually cajoled her into waiting for Trebin's answer.

Sometimes everything depends on keeping still, said Blur.

The next morning, Stisele went for practice with Govril, and he gave her a wooden practice weapon of her own, a saber just the right length and weight for her. She took it in her hand and knew its purpose—not speed or blood or fear, like the purposes of some of the metal weapons she'd polished, but knowledge. She spent that day beginning to unlearn what her shoulder joint used to be for, and learning all over again what an arm was. She couldn't let on about what she'd heard, couldn't ask, couldn't even thank Govril for his offer. Instead, she thought saber thoughts, thought with her hands about purpose.

"Different," said Govril at the end of the morning's session, and Stisele looked down and burned with shame. "Different but not wrong. I'll figure you out yet, Stisele of

Imlen." The bells chimed noon across the water. "You'll be eating with Nethrenilorhem today."

Stisele caught herself before she could ask why, and saved the question for the physician. Nethrenilorhem's rooms were exceptionally bright, and wherever there wasn't a window in the wall, there was a deep cabinet or a drawer labeled in Old Jhislaini. Lunch was set out for her and her host in his sitting room, and his big picture book was on the table.

"I liked it," she said. "Thank you."

"Most welcome. Have a seat."

"Why am I here?"

"That is the sort of question the Efa scholars like to ask. You have the mind to be a scholar, Stisele, but it has never seemed to me that you have the temperament."

"No, why am I *here*, silly." She buttered her bread thickly and stickied her hands.

He smiled. "Of course. I must ask you, as a matter of professional interest, about the day you cursed Jrene."

"She was asking for it."

"Yes, and she's accustomed to getting everything she asks for, isn't she? Mustn't disappoint the most important child in Beltresa, eh? But that's not the question that concerns me. Do you still see your imaginary friends?" And then he calmly set about eating his asparagus, as if he expected a long answer.

Stisele's heart beat fast. "Clevi says nobody wants to hear about that kind of thing. I'm seven, and it's not cute anymore."

"But I do want to hear. You can tell, because I'm asking. Do you still see your imaginary friends? Do they talk to you?"

Flash and Blur thought Nethrenilorhem was all right, and they'd always told her not to lie to physicians. But they'd told her not to get caught spying, too. And now that she needed them, they weren't here to tell her what to do. "Are you going to tell on me?"

"Have you done something wrong?"

"Clevi told me not to think about them anymore."

"But you do." It was a simple declaration, and he went back to eating.

"I still see them."

"Do they look like they used to?"

"Yeah."

"Still buzzy?"

"Only when they're talking."

He looked around the room. "Are they here now?"

"They don't go to lessons with me, now that I'm at the armory."

The physician looked thoughtful. "Maybe that's safer for Govril."

"Why?"

Nethrenilorhem set down his fork. "The day you were born, you were in terrible trouble. The Crown Contract forbade that your mother should live, once we'd got a look at you and knew for certain what your father was. Your father, well..."

"My mother's family had already killed him."

He raised his eyebrows. "Who told you that?"

"Flash did."

"One of your imaginary friends." And then his eyebrows curled tight against one another in puzzlement.

"Yeah."

The physician looked down at his big hands. "Did they tell you what I had to agree to, for you to live out the day?"

Stisele just stared blankly at him. She had no idea what he was talking about.

"In Jhislain, there are two colleges for two healing arts, and each art has its price. A long time ago, courtesans were just physicians with a specialty, and we had one lore together. Many, many years ago. Now, though, we physicians pay the price by carrying pain for our patients. The courtesans pay with their fertility. Barrenness is built into the stones of their college, and no one who stays to complete the training can ever have children."

What did any of this have to do with Stisele? "I'm going to be a soldier," she reminded him.

He sighed. "But you will never be a mother."

"Of course not. I can't ever get married. The Crown Contract says no miscegenation, and I'm already mixed up."

"That didn't stop your parents. Which was one of the things everyone was afraid of. That if you and people like you lived, there would someday be commoners who could kin-curse the Crown, or cross-bred aristocrats who would do it on behalf of the commons. Utroneth was willing to take the risk that you might curse your more distant kin in Ambra and the other Houses, in order to have her weapon against your closer kin in the House of Imlen. She thinks—I don't know if she's right or wrong—that close kinship makes for stronger curses, and you're as close as she can get to the ruler of Imlen. Ambra's House elders were willing to let her gamble on her ability to raise you, but they wanted assurances that there would be no others. Her Royal Highness put the proposition to me bluntly: If I struck you barren forever, you could live, and if I did not or could not strike you barren, the good of the Crown demanded that you die." He paused and looked at her, but she was too stunned to interrupt him with questions, so he went on. "The lore was in the oldest books, then. The College of Physicians has since suppressed it. What I did was a terrible wrong, to strike an infant barren on the day of her birth. I confessed my crime in writing to the First Among Equals of the College of Physicians and to the Elector of Jhislain, and will never see home again, but I could not be the reason an infant was murdered. So you live in captivity, and I live in exile. Here we are, alive. Lucky us. But there are always effects." He paused to pick at his salmon with his fork.

Paused so long, Stisele couldn't wait. "What effects?"

"When courtesans in training sacrifice their fertility, the power doesn't leave them; it is diverted, you could say. It changes form. The form it takes is shaped by their training. But I worked that sacrifice on you in a single day, and there was no training to shape it. I always wondered where the power would go. Apparently, it was diverted into hearing the dead, or something of that sort. We know so little about the dead, I can't guess any better than that yet."

"But Flash and Blur aren't dead. I was just talking to them this morning." She was terribly afraid for them all of a sudden. "Did you hurt them?"

"No, no. I couldn't find them if I wanted to. Your parents had their proper funeral rites. They were ash on the wave long ago."

"What does that have to do with Flash and Blur?"

He sat there quietly, until she saw it. And then she had to run to his washroom to be sick.

She was sick for a while, but she wouldn't ask him for help. He'd done something bad. Nonetheless, when he came with a cool, damp cloth to put on the back of her neck, she let him. The world was spinning.

"Maybe I shouldn't have told you."

"Why?"

"So many whys. I told you because soon you may be going away, and I didn't know if I would ever have another chance to ask you about them. Or to tell you the truth about what I'd done. But maybe I should have let you figure it out for yourself. Or let them tell you."

"But why?" It was so big.

"We all do the best we can, the best way we know how. I did what I could for your mother, I did what I could for you. What it means...maybe after we die, we find out. Or maybe not. Ask your parents why. No doubt they know things I don't." He was so serious, so sad. "I wish I could ask them things, ask you things about them, but it would not be wise to call attention to the little bit that you and I understand. If the House elders were not already a greater danger, then we would still have the Efa scholars to worry about. They like knowing things, and you know things already that no one else does. Probably no one else. If the Emperor of Efa sent his spies to snatch you, I'm not sure the Order could stop them. There's nothing like you in the records of the College of Physicians. And I hope there never is."

"I want to go to my room." She just wanted to see them, see that they were still all right.

"I volunteered to be the one to tell you other news, about your room. No one will wonder that we spoke, or that you are upset, or what we talked about. They think they already know."

"What?"

"Your room is not your room anymore. It is not safe for you to be near Jrene."

"Because she'll curse me back?"

"Because you might curse her again, and what all the people of the Crown, in all seven Houses of the Crown, fear more than anything else, more even than the Emperor of Efa, is the unknown potential of your curse. It pains me to instruct you so, but you must never let your mother's people see you look fondly on your father's people. The Old Beltresins have many grievances, and if ever it looks as if you will take their part and curse the aristocracy on Old Beltresa's behalf, that will be the end of you."

When she'd cleaned herself up, he showed her to her new quarters—a hastily cleared closet between Govril's rooms and the dormitory for the best of the big kids, the ones training up to be in Ambra's House levy to fight the Efa. Stisele had only had a few things she really cared about, and they were all there, hanging on pegs or set out on a tiny table.

Most importantly, Flash and Blur were lolling about on the little cot. Flash bounced to greet her and said, *Looks like we can't stay out of the armory altogether, after all.*

At first, Stisele felt a rush of relief—they were all right, and she would be all right. They'd look out for her, and there were two familiar things that could never be taken away. But then she looked at Flash and thought, *My father.* Her commoner father, Palan the scrivener. The reason everything was wrong with her.

Blur asked, *What is it?* Blur, Stisele's mother, the little fool who'd betrayed her whole people because she couldn't keep her legs together—that was what Clevi called Auscla of Imlen in the cautionary tale, every time it needed telling.

There was nobody but Nethrenilorhem to hear, so Stisele whispered, "I'm not talking to you. You're dead."

The little clouds of golden light recoiled at her anger and huddled closer to one another.

"They're here?" asked Nethrenilorhem.

"Of course. It's not like can get rid of them."

"I'm so sorry," he said very quietly into the former closet. "She needed to know. As far as I'm concerned, no one else needs to."

Stisele slammed the door on them. "I have to go to practice," she said. She wasn't going to cry one tear over her dead parents. Not one tear. She never had, and she wouldn't now, especially not in front of them. Everything was all their fault. No one followed her to her afternoon's polishing. Not the living, not the dead.

Govril was already waiting for her there. "The dormitories are full," he said.

"Yes, sir."

"You and I are the only people in this wing of the palace with solitary quarters. Highest and lowest. It's a funny world."

He was in an afternoon lesson mood, and she knew she was invited to ask him questions, but she was afraid she would cry. "It's not all that funny, sir."

"Maybe not."

"Will I get to see Samren and Clevi? If I don't go anywhere near my sister?"

"After you eat in the refectory, you may have an hour to do as you please, provided you stay away from the heir. You're too young for the books the other cadets work with at that hour."

"Thank you, sir."

"Have you ever trued an arrow before?"

"No, sir."

"Today, you're truing arrows." So he showed her how to spin them between her hands to see where they'd bent, and how to warm them and ease them and test them straight again. When he was satisfied he could leave her to her task and turn his attention to barking at the other cadets, she had hours to herself.

Many of the arrows were confused about their purposes, and some of them had no sense of purpose at all. "Who made *you?*" she asked them. "Bad job." They looked fine, but they were never going to fly right until they knew what they were about. They couldn't tell her, so she guessed and tried to tell them. Arrows were about speed, of course, and direction. They were Mommy Utroneth's personal sigil and her sorrow, for she'd seized the throne by turning her House's levy of archers against dead Mocred's useless child heir and her know-nothing regent, right on the parade ground in front of everybody. Stisele had heard the story from Utroneth herself—treason for the good of the Crown, for Beltresa would surely have fallen to the Efa had the city been left to the rule of a child of six and a pack of sycophants. The day Stisele had been told the story, she'd gone around asking all the grown-ups to explain what a sycophant was, but they had laughed nervously and dodged the question.

The pile of arrows was mostly done when Flash bumbled into the room.

"I see you. Go away." And she recited the weapons clause of the Crown Contract. Even dead, her father was still a commoner, and he was not to touch anything in the room.

What you're doing with your hands, he said, *putting the purpose in—I can teach you that.*

"You never trued an arrow in your life."

You know that's not what I mean. She ignored him, and he let her be until the last of the arrows was done, when he said, *They can't do this, you know. The Crownfolk, those up-jumped pirates. They have the weathercalling, but not the hand-sight. It's an advantage. They don't even know what it is.*

"And I bet you want me to keep that a secret, too."

We all keep it secret. Each Guild has its methods, secret even from one another. Maybe you'd have been a good blacksmith, or a woodwright. You'd have made a terrible scrivener, and I don't know the secrets of other Guilds. But the basics I can give you. Best to do it now while you're little. For most of us Old Beltresins it gets harder when we grow up.

"Don't say 'most of us' about me. I'm not a commoner. I get to true arrows."

Suit yourself. But you'd be a better weapon for the Princess if you learned it.

It was mean of him to tempt her like that. She didn't rise to the bait that day, but knowing she someday would only made her angrier.

For the whole week, she barely spoke to Flash and Blur. Palan and Auscla. Whoever they were. She hated them, and she could barely sleep at night because they might be in the tiny room with her, somewhere under the furniture or hiding behind the clothes that hung on the pegs.

Her one great comfort was that, in the lengthening spring evenings, Samren met her to play in the gardens. Under the approving eyes of Mommy Utroneth's courtiers, Stisele and Samren conducted naval battles mapped out with stones on the grass, and planned cavalry assaults with the army of little wooden people he carried in a cotton sack. Stisele had to take her comfort in Samren's company because Clevi and Utroneth had no time for her, and nobody would tell her why.

The next fifthday, she knew her week of waiting was up. Today, Mommy Utroneth would get some kind of answer from Trebin of Ythrae. Someone would decide something, and Stisele's whole life might change again. Or end. She wasn't all that scared about it, and when she caught sight of Blur's bright edges sticking out under the hem of her overshirt where it hung on its peg, Stisele realized why not. All her life, she'd been keeping company with dead people. What was there to be afraid of? If things went badly for her, she'd be like her parents. With her parents. That didn't seem so horrible.

But then, they spent all their time worrying about how to keep her alive, so they probably knew something she didn't. They knew things even Nethrenilorhem didn't know, which was hard to imagine, because he knew more than anybody else Stisele had ever met. She wished she could ask them. It wouldn't be so hard. Blur was right there, hiding under the overshirt, and it was time for Stisele to get dressed anyway. But she was still mad at them, so she pulled the overshirt off the peg abruptly and pretended not to notice as Blur sped straight down the wall to cram herself into Stisele's left boot. But then Stisele had to put her boots on, and Blur tickled her foot on the way out through the lacing. Stisele didn't want to laugh.

She missed them so much.

When the morning was half spent, and she'd practiced standing in all the new ways to stand for a while, one of Emnir of Gorsae's underlings in the Order came to the armory door. He stood there in his dress blacks, all graceful layers and silver ornament. "Stisele of Imlen," he said.

"Yes?"

"Follow me."

Govril nodded his permission, so Stisele went.

Flash clung close to her, and Blur drifted across the surface of the agent in black—sniffing him all over, that was what it looked like. *I can't tell what he wants,* she said. And Flash trembled.

"Excuse me, sir," said Stisele.

The agent looked down at her as they walked. "What is it?"

"Where are we going?"

"To the dock."

That might mean anything, said Blur. *Ask him some more.*

But Stisele smiled. "Am I going somewhere?"

"My instructions are to take you to the dock."

Flash said, *You can swim for it, if it comes to that. We might be able to help. Water's different.*

Stisele ignored her father. She skipped down the ornate mirrored corridor, and the agent had to hurry his pace a little to keep up with her. He needed that brisk pace all across the greensward and down the steps carved into the rock face. Where the water beat against the steelwood pilings, the two of them stopped together.

A servant waited there with a large wooden trunk carved with Imlen's House insignia. He was an uncommonly broad-shouldered servant. Stisele wondered if he'd carried the trunk down those tricky stone steps alone.

Hey, said Blur, *that's mine. Was mine.* She slid into the keyhole, and her muffled voice inside the trunk said, *They gave you some spare pairs of boots.*

Flash rolled across the planks to examine the trunk. *Well,* he said, *I suppose they wouldn't have made you new boots if they meant to do you in.*

So Stisele would be well provisioned, wherever she was going. She'd thank Mommy Utroneth, whenever the Princess showed up to see her off.

The black-clad agent stood at ease, watching her. She wandered around the dock, carefully avoiding him and the servant, but eventually boredom took hold, and she tried to open the trunk.

"Stop," said the agent.

"Yes, sir." When was Mommy Utroneth coming?

Stisele looked up when she heard rowers singing a chantey, "Spires of Beltresa," and their oars pulled at the waves. It was Ythrae's old royal barge, with old Prince Calnir's own seal carved into it. Trebin himself stood in the prow, his hair pulled back severely, his moustache waxed into improbable curlicues.

Ridiculous affectation, said Blur.

Today, said Flash, *I'm not inclined to knock it.*

Ythrae's rowers threw a line to the servant, who threw a line from the dock back across to them, and they gave "Spires of Beltresa" one more chorus while they made fast what was loose.

At long last, Trebin said, "Good morning, Stisele."

She stood at attention. "Good morning, sir."

"Are you ready to see the world?"

One last time, Stisele looked around the dock. "She's not going to say goodbye to me, is she?"

"It would hardly be goodbye," he said. "Her Royal Highness has given me a...very extensive list of her expectations regarding your upbringing, many of which concern visits. If she has not come, then there must be a dire matter of state that demands her attention."

"A dire matter of state." Stisele thought those words to herself a few more times, until they didn't mean anything. She stood hesitantly on the dock. Never before had she crossed water to any other place. She'd stood here waving goodbye to her siblings and Mommy Utroneth when they'd taken the House of Ambra's delicate, refined barge to the city, and wished so many times that she could go with them. This wasn't the same thing, not at all. Riding this gaudy old barge with a trusted retainer was nothing like traveling as her Mommy's daughter.

Going with Trebin was like saying it would never happen that way.

She would not cry in front of Trebin. Not even in the little way she was practicing. "Do I have to go?"

"Do I have to go, what?"

"Do I have to go, sir?"

"This is the last moment when you can choose. Go to the city with me, as my particular pupil, and obey me in all things, and see the world. Or turn back now, and you will probably never leave Ambra Islet."

That was all Stisele needed to hear. She ran across the gangplank onto the barge so fast she bumped right into Harentil. Hadn't even seen her.

"Hello again," Harentil said.

Stisele remembered what she'd heard Trebin say— something about having a daughter who had never wanted to be an only child. For the first time, Stisele thought the words *my sister,* and something other than resentment of Jrene went with the words. Everything was upside down. All she managed to say was, "Hello."

Trebin made some hand gesture to the chief rower, and the barge hove away from the dock. Stisele ran, then, to stand in the prow of the barge and watch the city draw nearer. The rowers pulled in perfect unison, and the distance between Stisele and her parents' city fell away. The spires she'd been taught to sing about rose from the waves, just like in the song. As long as she could remember, they'd been pretty toys Jrene got to play with that Stisele could never touch. Now those spires rose high above her, and the barge cut under the white marble expanse of Laddercrew Bridge between the gull-ridden Point Quay tip of Morningside and the ornately carved façade of the Fire Brigade's headquarters on Southedge.

She was *in* the city now, surrounded by it, and after another turn up the canal, the island called Calnir's Prize came clear. It must be Calnir's Prize, for surely those were palaces, three of them in a row up the convex curve of an island wrapped in stone quays.

Carved into one quay was Ythrae's House sigil, and that was where the barge docked. Stisele waited until Trebin and Harentil stepped across the few little inches of canal between the barge and the stone, and she waited until he commanded her to cross.

She set foot in the city now. Hers, just like her parents always told her it would be. Her arms prickled up in gooseflesh.

"This," said Trebin, "is Ythrae Palace, where you will live." The whole place was a blur to her, though he tried to show her around. He introduced her to so many people, she lost count, and he finally gave up telling her more names.

They left Harentil in Ythrae's nursery, and Trebin led Stisele to the landward side of the palace, where they stepped into a glossily lacquered palanquin that had burly servants to carry it. She leaned her head out the window to watch the life of the city walking by her—courtiers promenading down the boulevard, city guardsmen in gray and liveried servants in the colors of every House and embassy, and Crown-born Guild Allies in the waist-coats that named their Guild affiliations, and Guildfolk themselves—commoners who walked with their heads held high even on Calnir's Prize. The palanquin jounced with every synchronized step of the bearers, and Stisele bumped her head on the windowframe as she leaned out to stare in open-mouthed wonder.

"This," said Trebin, "is Beltresa, which your mother and I live to serve."

Every time Stisele thought of a question to ask, another came to her and drove the last one right out of her head.

Blur shimmered beside her. *Close your mouth, darling. We are not a codfish.*

Stisele closed her mouth.

When the palanquin arrived at the old Royal Palace, where Mommy Utroneth kept her administrators, the bearers carried it straight through a minor doorway into a courtyard, and then into a chain of linked courtyards, until they reached a stable. There, the bearers set the palanquin down and opened the glossy door. Trebin stepped out, and Stisele followed.

"Is this where I'll train?"

"Only for the merest beginning," he said. "These horses don't know much more than ceremony. Ceremony's good, but I look forward to the day I can take you to the Upriver garrisons. Upriver and out, Stisele, that's where our empire's headed."

She was so high up—almost as high as she'd ever been in her apple tree—
she was a spire of Beltresa rising from the waves.

"But it's Efa with the Empire."

Trebin smiled. "We'll see about that. Come on."

There were young men and women all around them, wearing the uniforms of all the different Houses' troop levies. They saluted Trebin as he passed. Finally, he reached a young woman who led a black horse—it seemed impossibly big. "This," said Trebin, "is the horse you'll learn on." He set his hands on either side of Stisele's waist and lifted her up as if she weighed nothing at all, then set her down on the saddle.

She felt as if she were straddling a dinner table. Her muscles, still sore from the stances Govril of Ambra had been teaching her, lit up with pain right away, but she didn't care. She was on a real horse, and the real horse's reins were in Trebin's hands, and the real horse's hooves were on the ancient cobblestones of Beltresa, on Calnir's Prize itself. She was so high up—almost as high as she'd ever been in her apple tree—she was a spire of Beltresa rising from the waves.

ABOUT THE AUTHOR

S arah Avery's collection of contemporary fantasy novellas, *Tales from Rugosa Coven,* won the 2015 Mythopoeic Fantasy Award. She grew up as an Army brat in Kentucky and Korea, Japan and Germany, with a long stretch near Washington, D.C. An escaped academic, she wrote her doctoral dissertation on modernist poetry before returning to her first love, writing fantasy. Her short stories have appeared in *Jim Baen's Universe* and *Fantasy Scroll,* as well as *Black Gate,* where she has been a columnist for many years. With David Sklar she coedited the themed anthology *Trafficking in Magic, Magicking in Traffic.* She lives in Maryland with her husband and sons.

CPSIA information can be obtained at www.ICGtesting.com
Printed in the USA
BVOW04s0414240916

463175BV00001B/1/P